By Brigitte Weninger

# Zara Zebra Counts

### Illustrated by Anna Laura Cantone

A Michael Neugebauer Book
NORTH-SOUTH BOOKS
New York/London

Zara Zebra has some candy.
How many pieces of candy does
she have?
That's too much candy for **1** little zebra!

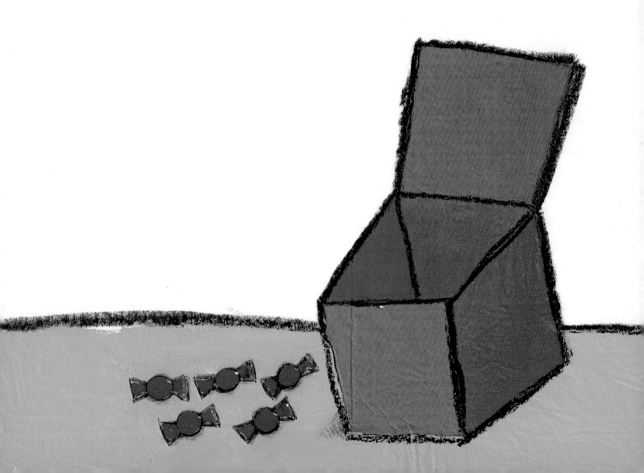

Zara Zebra invites Bear to share
the candy.
But there's still too much candy
for **2** friends.

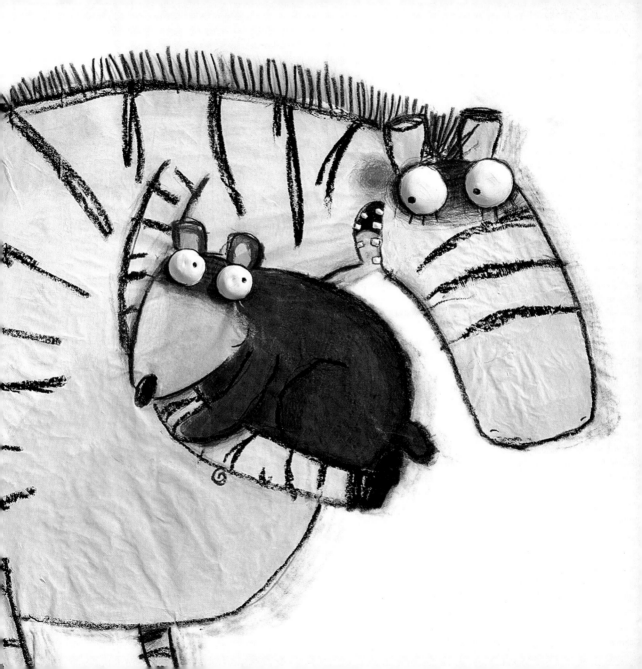

Zara Zebra and Bear ask Duck
to share the candy.
But there's still too much candy
for **3** friends.

Zara Zebra and Bear and Duck ask Crocodile to share the candy. But there's still too much candy for **4** friends.

So Zara Zebra and Bear and Duck and Crocodile ask Kitty to share the candy. Now there are **5** friends.